This book belongs to:

Lydia Rose

EVERYTHING NAOMI LOVED

EVERYTHING NAOMI LOVED

Written by
Katie Yamasaki & **Ian Lendler**

Illustrated by
Katie Yamasaki

Norton Young Readers • An Imprint of W. W. Norton & Company • *Independent Publishers Since 1923*

For Pop—K.Y.

Text copyright © 2020 by Katie Yamasaki and Ian Lendler
Illustrations copyright © 2020 by Katie Yamasaki

Printed in China
First Edition

For information about permission to reproduce selections from this book, write to
Permissions, W. W. Norton & Company, Inc., 500 Fifth Avenue, New York, NY 10110

For information about special discounts for bulk purchases, please contact
W. W. Norton Special Sales at specialsales@wwnorton.com or 800-233-4830

Manufacturing by Toppan Leefung
Book design by Aram Kim
Production manager: Julia Druskin

Library of Congress Cataloging-in-Publication Data

Names: Yamasaki, Katie, author, illustrator. | Lendler, Ian, author.
Title: Everything Naomi loved / written by Katie Yamasaki & Ian Lendler ; illustrated by Katie Yamasaki.
Description: First edition. | New York, NY : Norton Young Readers, [2020] | Audience: Ages 4–8. |
    Summary: Naomi has always loved her vibrant neighborhood but things are changing quickly so,
    inspired by Mr. Ray, she paints murals to preserve her favorite memories.
Identifiers: LCCN 2019052255 | ISBN 9781324004912 (hardcover) | ISBN 9781324004929 (epub)
Subjects: CYAC: City and town life—Fiction. | Neighborhoods—Fiction. | Loss (Psychology)—Fiction. |
    Mural painting and decoration—Fiction.
Classification: LCC PZ7.Y19157 Eve 2020 | DDC [E]—dc23
LC record available at https://lccn.loc.gov/2019052255

W. W. Norton & Company, Inc., 500 Fifth Avenue, New York, N.Y. 10110
www.wwnorton.com

W. W. Norton & Company Ltd., 15 Carlisle Street, London W1D 3BS

1 2 3 4 5 6 7 8 9 0

When Naomi wanted
to see the world
she looked out her window . . .

. . . onto 11th Street.
It wasn't pretty
but it was alive!

It had everything:
Mister Ray's Automotive.
Pizza by the slice.
$1 wash!
Hair by Carmen.
Honking, blaring, booming cars,
and the corner bodega.
Lotto tix! Coffee! Ices! Fruit!

It had nature
and her best friend, Ada.

Every afternoon
while their parents worked,
Naomi and Ada scooted up
and scooted down.

In the summer,
in the shade of the tree,
they took sidewalk chalk
and drew a forest
and tamed the wild animals that roamed by.
The Naomi and Ada 11th Street Safari!

By the time their parents came back from work
Naomi and Ada were tired.
Their parents were tired.
Those nights, Naomi and her mom and dad
wished the tree and the neon lights
and the never-ending hum of cars
and Ada
goodnight.

Sweet dreams, 11th Street.

One day, Naomi woke up and the tree was gone.
"They're building something new," said her mom.
"Something fancy," said her dad.

¡pura Vida!
Bodega
Coffee·Candy

RAY

"But I loved that tree," said Naomi.
Suddenly, 11th Street looked concrete and gray.

Mister Ray thought so, too.
So he got some brushes
and paint from his shop.
He touched a brush to the wall
and something started to grow.

"Things change," he said,
"But where I grew up
when something we love goes away
we paint it on the wall
so it's always with us.
Do you want to help?"
Naomi shook her head.
She had never seen
Mister Ray paint before.
He was so good
she didn't want to ruin it.

When he was done,
11th Street got its green back.

A few weeks later, Ada buzzed . . .
. . . but not to play.
It was to say goodbye.
Her family was moving.
Their building was being torn down.
Just like that, Naomi's
best friend was gone.

The next morning, Naomi had no one to play with.
So she picked up her sidewalk chalk
and drew a scooter on the wall.
"You want some help?" asked Mister Ray.
"Yes, please," said Naomi.

So he showed her how to paint a foot,
and a leg,
and a summer dress.
"Ada," said Naomi.
"Not yet," said Mister Ray.
They made the last touch—Ada's smile.
And Naomi couldn't help it,
she smiled too.

But 11th Street changed more and more.

Shops closed. Signs went up.

Coming Soon! Luxury Living!

And one day Mister Ray hung a sign of his own.

Closed for Good

"Things change," he said.
"Help me say goodbye."

Together, they took out the paint.
Mister Ray painted a rectangle
that turned into a window
and in that window . . .

"Hey!" said Naomi. "That's me!"
"That's what I'll remember," said Mister Ray.
"My view every day for the last eight years."
All that time looking out at 11th Street.
Naomi never realized she was part of it.
He asked, "What do you see out your window?"

She said, "I see you every morning."
So Mister Ray painted himself waving.
¡Hola!
It looked a bit different though.
"You don't have that much hair," said Naomi.
"Like I said," replied Mister Ray,
"I'm remembering."

He handed her his brushes.
"Things change," said Naomi.
That's how they said goodbye.

Soon, everyone on 11th Street was saying goodbye.
Whether they wanted to or not.
Now, when Naomi looked out her window
she didn't see her world.

COMING
SOON
chic City Living

11th Street
From
Above
coming
soon

your style
city
new
address

12th
Street

So Naomi took Mister Ray's brush
and everything that 11th Street lost,
everything she loved,

she remembered on the wall.

The pizza smell.
Baseball on the bodega radio.
The laundromat's soap and steam.
Cherry ice from Mrs. Sanchez.
Even the daydreams
under the tree
with her best friend
on 11th Street.

Then the workers in hard hats came
with big machines.
They put a fence in front of her wall.
They came to make a change.

Naomi's world was gone . . .

. . . but she kept a little piece.

And when her family moved,
that piece stayed with her,
from 11th Street . . .

. . . all the way to 111th Street.
It wasn't pretty.
But Naomi knew,
things change.
It's not easy.

But when we find places
to call home
and people to love . . .

. . . a new world will grow.